This is for you, Mom,
with love

– GH

tiger tales
an imprint of ME Media, LLC
202 Old Ridgefield Road, Wilton, CT 06897
Published in the United States 2004
Originally published in Great Britain 2004
By Little Tiger Press
An imprint of Magi Publications
Text copyright © 2004 Jane Johnson
Illustrations copyright © 2004 Gaby Hansen
CIP data is available
ISBN 1-58925-043-5
Printed in Singapore
1 3 5 7 9 10 8 6 4 2

Little Bunny's Bathtime!

by Jane Johnson

Illustrated by Gaby Hansen

tiger tales

"Bathtime for my little rabbits!" called Mrs. Rabbit, and her children came running. All except her youngest little one.

"I don't want a bath,"
said Little Bunny. "I want
to keep playing."

"You really want to play all by yourself?"
asked Mrs. Rabbit. Little Bunny nodded, but
now he wasn't so sure.

"Well, you be good while I'm busy with the others," said Mrs. Rabbit, plopping her bunnies into the bathtub.

"Swish, splish, splash," sang
the little rabbits happily,
swirling their bubbles around.
Little Bunny wanted
to play, too.

"Look at me!" he called,
hiding behind the towels.

"Yes, dear," said Mrs. Rabbit, but
she went on washing the others.
"Tickly, wiggly, giggly toes," sang
the little rabbits as they wiggled their
feet in the water.

"Guess where I am?"
shouted Little Bunny,
hidden in the
laundry basket.

"Found you," smiled
his mother, lifting the lid.

But she turned back to
finish washing the others.

"Out you go," puffed Mrs. Rabbit,
lifting her children out of the tub.

"Rub-a-dub-dub, you've all had a scrub," she laughed. "What lovely, clean bunnies you are!"

Little Bunny was upset.
He wanted his mommy
to notice him.

So he climbed up…

and up…as far as he
could. But suddenly…

SPLASH!

He fell into the bathtub!

"Oh my!" cried Mrs. Rabbit, scooping
him out of the water right away.

Little Bunny gazed up at her happily.
"I'm ready for my bath now, Mommy,"
he said, smiling sweetly.

Mrs. Rabbit couldn't
help smiling back.
    "Off you go to play
quietly," she said to
her other rabbits.

Then she ran
fresh water and
gave Little Bunny
his own special bath.

"Soapy ears and soapy toes, and soapy little bunny nose!" sang Mrs. Rabbit. She washed his ears while he played with the new bubbles.

"I love you, Mommy," said Little Bunny.

"I love you, too, sweetheart!"

She washed his back while he played with his boat.

"You're the best mommy in the whole world," said Little Bunny.

"And you're my precious little bunnykin."

She dried his fur and whiskers, and said, "Mmm, you smell so nice and clean!"

And Little Bunny kissed his mommy and hugged her tight.

"There now, all done," sighed Mrs. Rabbit. "It's time for bed. Where are my other little rabbits?"

She found them in the kitchen.
"Oh no! What a mess!" cried
Mrs. Rabbit. "You're all dirty again.
You all need another bath!"

"Yes," giggled Little Bunny.
"All except me!"